A ROOKIE READER

PAUL
THE
PITCHER

Written and Illustrated
By Paul Sharp

D1374128

Children's Press®
A Division of Scholastic Inc.
New York • Toronto • London • Auckland • Sydney
Mexico City • New Delhi • Hong Kong
Danbury, Connecticut

Rookie
READY TO
LEARN

Dear Parents/Educators,

Welcome to Rookie Ready to Learn. Each Rookie Reader in this series includes additional age-appropriate Let's Learn Together activity pages that help your young child to be better prepared when starting school. *Paul the Pitcher* offers opportunities for you and your child to talk about the important social/emotional skill of pride in accomplishment.

Here are early-learning skills you and your child will encounter in the *Paul the Pitcher* Let's Learn Together pages:

• Rhyming
• Measurement
• Vocabulary

We hope you enjoy sharing this delightful, enhanced reading experience with your early learner.

Library of Congress Cataloging-in-Publication Data

Sharp, Paul.
  Paul the pitcher / written and illustrated by Paul Sharp.
    p. cm. -- (Rookie ready to learn)
  Summary: Rhymed text describes the different things Paul enjoys when
he throws a ball. Includes suggested learning activities.
  ISBN 978-0-531-26426-3 -- ISBN 978-0-531-26651-9 (pbk.)
[1. Stories in rhyme. 2. Baseball--Fiction.] I. Title. II. Series
  PZ8.3.S532Pau 2011
  [E]--dc22

                                                        2010049996

© 2011 by Scholastic Inc.
Illustrations © 2011 Paul Sharp
All rights reserved.
Printed in the United States of America. 113

1 2 3 4 5 6 7 8 9 10 R 18 17 16 15 14 13 12 11

Paul the pitcher throws a ball.

3

Baseball is the game for Paul.

Paul the pitcher throws a ball.

He throws the ball
from spring till fall.

9

He throws it to the catcher's mitt,

unless the batter gets a hit.

Paul the pitcher loves to throw,

sometimes high,

sometimes low.

Paul the pitcher loves to throw,

sometimes fast,

sometimes slow.

To throw the ball is lots of fun,

22

23

24

unless the batter gets a run.

Paul the pitcher loves to throw.

Someday he'd like to be a pro.

Congratulations!

You just finished reading *Paul the Pitcher* and learned about something Paul likes — baseball.

<hr />

About the Author/Illustrator

Paul Sharp graduated from the Art Institute of Pittsburgh with a degree in Visual Communications. He has done illustrations for numerous children's books and magazines. This is the fifth book Paul has illustrated for Children's Press. He also wrote it. Paul presently lives, and works as an artist, in Lafayette, Indiana.

Paul the Pitcher

Let's learn together!

Take Me Out to Play Ball

(Sing the song below to the tune
of "Take Me Out to the Ball Game.")

Take me out
to the ball game,
Take me out
with the crowd.
I'll show you how
I'm becoming a pro.
It took some time to
perfect my throw.
Let's go, go, go to the
playground,
So I can practice all day.
For it's one, two, three
strikes you're out
And I'll say *hip, hip, hooray*!

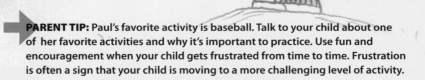

PARENT TIP: Paul's favorite activity is baseball. Talk to your child about one of her favorite activities and why it's important to practice. Use fun and encouragement when your child gets frustrated from time to time. Frustration is often a sign that your child is moving to a more challenging level of activity.

Rhyme Time

Many words in *Paul the Pitcher* rhyme, such as *ball* and *fall*.
Rhyming words have the same ending sounds.

Look at a picture in the top row. Find and point to the word that rhymes with it in the bottom row.

cat

truck

goat

boat

duck

bat

PARENT TIP: Have more fun rhyming. Challenge your child to see how many other words he can come up with that rhyme with *cat* and *bat*.

Near or Far?

Three batters are on the run. Rulers are used to measure distance. Look at the ruler below. The distance between each number equals one inch. How far did the first batter go? The second? The third?

PARENT TIP: Using the ruler in the book, kids can measure other objects, such as a crayon or a wooden block. You can reinforce the concept of measurement by using words such as *shorter/taller*, *smaller/larger*, *near/far*, etc., in everyday conversations with your child.

35

Batter Up!

You don't have to head outside to practice your baseball swing.

You can do it right at home. Use an empty paper towel tube as the bat. Then make a ball out of aluminum foil. You'll be ready to hit a home run in no time!

PARENT TIP: For children to feel confident, focus on their strength. Make sure you let them know that strengths can come in different forms — characteristics like kindness and generosity; academic, artistic, athletic, or musical skills; or even a sense of humor.

Rookie
READY TO
LEARN

When I Grow Up

Finish this rhyming poem about what you want to be by saying the missing word in each sentence.

When I look to the future,
this is what I see:
A _____
is what I hope to be.

Hard work and
_____are the key
To become the best
possible me!

Paul the Pitcher Word List (38 Words)

a	fun	lots	someday
ball	game	loves	sometimes
baseball	gets	low	spring
batter	he	mitt	the
be	he'd	of	throw(s)
catcher's	high	Paul	till
fall	hit	pitcher	to
fast	is	pro	unless
for	it	run	
from	like	slow	

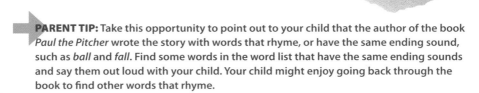

PARENT TIP: Take this opportunity to point out to your child that the author of the book *Paul the Pitcher* wrote the story with words that rhyme, or have the same ending sound, such as *ball* and *fall*. Find some words in the word list that have the same ending sounds and say them out loud with your child. Your child might enjoy going back through the book to find other words that rhyme.